Float On

LETIZIA
THERE ARE NO TRIPOD
STORIES PUBLISHED YET...
BUT THAT COULD
CHANGE.

Float On

Trent Ogilvie

Float On

Published in Canada by
Trent Ogilvie
Oakville, ON

Float On written and edited
by Trent Ogilvie

ISBN 978-1-927023-75-4

Printed and bound in the USA
Typeset and cover image by Trent Ogilvie
Edited by Patricia Ogilvie
and Alexander Tkachuk

For Dean.

Fourteen Mile Creek

Float On

Fourteen Mile Creek

The Chain Link Fence

"Hurry! If we get caught we'll be grounded for a week," my sister Megan, ten, said in October 1999, as she stepped across our backyard, in Oakville, Ontario, towards the chain link fence. I, eight, followed her. Behind the fence, large spruce trees ascended from the forest's damp soil and their peaks rose above our two-story brick house. A broken axe rested on the fence. Electrical wires skimmed the trees that edged our backyard. The wires merged at a wooden pole among the tree trunks. Megan and I reached the path, leapt across the stones, stopped in front of the chain link fence and stared into the forest. The first row of spruces reached over the chain link fence. Their pine-filled branches sheltered us from the October sun.

"They won't be mad when we tell them what we saw," I said.

"I'm telling you, Trent, there's nothing in there."

My small hands clasped the large, black binoculars that hung around my neck. I shoved their lenses towards my eyes, stared into the forest and saw a yellow and brown blur. My eyes stung, as my small fingertips found the focus dial on top of the binoculars and twisted it. After a moment, the black mold spots on the autumn leaves focused. I scanned the dead leaves, sighed and dropped the binoculars against my chest.

"There is too. I bet you we go out there and see all sorts of cool things," I said.

"Oh yeah? Like what?"

I turned towards the forest. An autumn breeze blew beneath the first row of spruces and caught my long, brown hair. My cheeks reddened.

"Like owls and falcons and vultures!" I squirmed. My eyes glistened.

Megan frowned.

"At *most* we'll see a squirrel."

Megan placed her hands on top of the chain-link fence, pushed her feet off the ground with her hands and flung her boots over the green chain-link spikes that lined the top of the fence. She landed on a pile of dead leaves. A crunch and crackle echoed into the backyard. Megan turned to me. Her eyebrow rose.

"Well, are you coming or what? This was your idea," she said.

My body shook, as my small hands gripped the binoculars.

I shifted towards the empty backyard and stared at our kitchen's glass door.

"Maybe Mom or Dad should be out here, you know, just in case something happens," I said.

"What're you talking about? Nothing's going to happen. Don't be a wimp. We'll be in and out quick. Now hurry up and hop over or I'm going in without you."

Megan turned from me and walked into the forest. I gazed back towards our house, sighed, tightened the binocular strap and stepped towards the fence. My body shivered. I reached my arms above my head and placed my small hands between two chain link spikes on top of the fence. I tried to pull my feet off the ground, but a pain seared from my armpits down to my hips. I stopped for a moment. My hands still held the top of the fence. I shoved my hiking boot into one of the chain links. I climbed. After a moment, I sat on top of the fence. One leg hung over the fence inside the backyard and the other hung over the fence inside the forest. I turned back to the house again, closed my eyes and shifted my weight towards the forest. My torso fell towards the forest floor and my pant leg caught a chain link spike. My pants tore. My torso landed on my binoculars. I whined. Megan walked over to me.

"What do you think you're doing?" she asked. I felt the hole in my jeans and sobbed.

"Mom's going to be mad at me, I ruined my jeans," I said, as tears formed in my eyes.

"She's going to be even madder if she finds out we went in the forest without asking, now hurry up before we get in real trouble."

Megan grabbed my hands and pulled me to my feet. She

brushed the dead leaves off my flannel sweater, wiped the dirt off my binocular lenses, held my hand and walked me a few feet into the forest. Dead leaves dissipated beneath my hiking boots, as my small hand trembled in hers. She nudged me.

"Look up there," Megan said. I followed her finger upwards. My tear-filled eyes stared at the tree branches. A small, brown object circled the sky.

"What is it? I can't see anything," I said.

Megan observed me.

"Wipe your eyes, and then look."

I rubbed my flannel sleeve across my eyes until the black mold spots on the dead leaves focused again, then I looked up. Orange and yellow leaves drifted towards the ground. A bird glided through the spruce trees, maple branches and blue sky. Its hooked yellow beak, black eyes, brown and white striped feathers, long talons and red tail feathers shimmered in the sunlight. I gasped, as I grabbed my binoculars and shoved them to my eyes.

"A bird! A bird!" I shouted.

"Shhh," Megan said, "we don't want to scare it."

I stared through my binoculars, twisted the dial on top until the dead leaves on the top branches focused, found the bird in the sky and studied its brown, white and red feathers.

"That's a red-tailed hawk," I said.

Megan squinted through the trees.

"How do you know?"

"Its tail feathers are red, duh. I saw them in a bird book. The map in the book said they're common around here. I told you, I knew we'd see something!"

Megan sighed, turned and walked towards the fence. The

chain link fence clinked. I stared at the hawk for a moment
longer through my binoculars. As a wind drifted between
the forest's trees, I turned and saw Megan sprint towards the
house. Our dad stood on the back deck. My heart beat against
my chest. A bird chirped.

The Tree by the Creek

Tears formed, as I dropped my fishing rod onto the slate beside Fourteen Mile Creek. I, nine, stared at the rod. The line tangled around the reel and thirty feet of it slumped across the water. My lower lip trembled. I turned, slid across the slate and ran into the forest.

Dead leaves crackled beneath my size four sneakers. Trees blurred. Tears glided across my temples and slithered into my brown mullet. I gawked at the green chain link fence at the top of the tree-covered hill. My foot sunk into the mud. As I fell, my hand grabbed a small tree trunk. I steadied myself and glowered at the grey bark on the tree. My small fingers squeezed the trunk. I glared at the tree.

"Get out of my way!" I shrieked. My small hand squeezed the trunk tighter and I felt the bark crumble beneath my fingers. I pushed the tree. Dead leaves rose, as the tree slammed onto the forest floor. Mold floated into the air. My nose twitched. I stared at the fallen tree trunk, the hole in the soil, then the tree trunk again. I gaped.

"Oh no," I said, as I observed the pieces of bark on my small fingers. I stepped back from the tree. A warm stream travelled across the dried tears on my cheeks. My lower lip trembled again. The worn-down treads on my sneakers slipped on the dry leaves, as I ran up the hill towards the chain-link fence.

"What's wrong, Trent?" a girl's voice asked. I stopped and saw a pile of sticks shaped like a tee pee. My sister Megan and her friend, Jane, sat inside. Jane's red hair shimmered through the tee pee.

"What's wrong, Trent?" Megan repeated. My mouth opened, closed, and opened again.

"My fishing rod… the tree… trouble…" My lips quivered. I ran up the rest of the hill. My torso and legs slammed into the chain-link fence. The fence rattled. I hopped over into my backyard. My sneakers sprinted across the cedar mulch garden and grass towards my house. I burst through the front door. My body fell onto the TV room couch. I stared at the popcorn ceiling.

I'm going to get arrested. I knocked over that tree. The police are going to find out. I left my broken fishing rod by the creek. They're going to know it was me.

My body shook and my lower lip covered my upper lip. The popcorn ceiling flattened. My eyes blurred.

The police will probably show up any minute and take me to jail.

I whimpered.

How will I tell mom?

A moment later, the front door creaked open. I flinched, turned over and slipped my head under a pillow.

"Trent?" a girl's voice asked. I pulled my head out from under the pillow and felt the static pull my hair up. Megan stared at me.

"Come here for a second," she said. I sighed, wiped my tears on my sweater sleeve and tottered out the front door with her. She pointed to the ground. My fishing rod rested on the stone walkway.

"You left it by the creek," she said, "the line was a little tangled so it wouldn't wind up, but I fixed it for you."

I gazed at the fishing rod. The line wound around the reel. "Thanks."

I smiled. Megan picked up the fishing rod, handed it to me and walked to the backyard. A moment later, the chain-link fence rattled. I stared at the fishing rod in my small hands and noticed pieces of bark still on my fingers. A car sped down the street. Its engine rumbled. I gulped.

The Ripples Beyond the Bridge

"Hurry, here they come! Grab your net, hurry!" Jamie, my
grade five friend, screamed, as he sprinted into Fourteen Mile
Creek in August 2001. I followed him. Water splashed inside
my pant legs. Brown water roared past my ankles. White foam
attached to my jeans. Rapids formed over jagged rocks, as
the water travelled under the old concrete bridge towards us.
Graffiti lined the bridge's cracked concrete walls. Cars passed
on Lakeshore Road on top of the bridge. In the still water
before the bridge, a splash shattered the brown surface. Jamie
pointed at the rippled water.

"See? Right there!" he said.

I squinted. My heart beat against my flannel shirt. I

clenched the small butterfly net. My small fingers sweat around the orange plastic handle.

"Man," Jamie said, "We're going to be the coolest grade five kids if we catch something."

"Do you think we'll catch something?"

Jamie looked at my net.

"Well, do *you* think you'll catch anything with that toy?"

I studied the thin opening and mesh on the net. The ripples increased beyond the bridge. A few splashes rose into the area closer to the rapids. I gripped my butterfly net tighter.

"It's all I had," I said.

"I bet you it breaks first try, if you can even get a hold of one with that tiny thing."

Jamie held his brand new fishing net into the air. The sun shimmered on the thick green mesh and the mesh fluttered around the large steel hole. Jamie swatted the net towards the water and the water splashed onto the shore.

"See how much area this thing covers? I guarantee you I snag ten before you hit one," Jamie said.

I sighed, as Jamie swatted the brown water again. Beneath the brown surface, water crept into my sneakers. My socks moistened. Small sediments gathered between my toes. I sighed again, as I stared at the ripples beyond the bridge. A car raced across the road above. The engine's rumble echoed across the creek and drowned beneath the rapid's roar.

Jamie swatted the water again. He froze. A moment later, a rough object slammed into my ankle. My ankle stung and I gasped. I looked at Jamie, Jamie looked at me. My eyes drifted to my ankles. The brown water hid my feet. A fish's brown head poked out through the surface. Black dots speckled its scales, and its scales glinted a dull brown in the sunlight. A large white snout protruded from its mouth. The fish drifted towards me. Its snout grasped my jeans. I flinched. A moment later, the fish swam, drifted into the rapids and tumbled against the rocks.

"Eww," I shrieked, "did you see that thing? What's on its face?"

Jamie jumped into the air, splashed into the brown water and jumped again. Water drops covered his pants and shirt. A moment later, another fish's brown head rose above the water. The fish stared at Jamie. Its white snout pushed towards his ankles.

"What are these things?" I asked.

Jamie slashed his net towards the water. A large burst of water sprayed into the air and landed beside me. Jamie shrieked and answered,

"Get away from me! What? I think – I said get! - They're called suckers?"

"Suckers?"

"Yes – get away! – Suckers."

The fish beside Jamie swam into the rapids too. Its body slammed into the rocks and its white snout sunk beneath the surface.

"How big do you think they are?" I asked.

"Probably about a foot and a half, maybe two."

Beneath the bridge, water soared into the air higher than the rapids. Waves covered the entire area between the creek's two shores. A sucker jumped into the air.

"How many of those gross things do you think are in that pack?" I asked.

"A thousand, maybe two thousand."

"Two thousand suckers?"

Jamie gasped and nodded.

"At least."

My small hands trembled around the butterfly net's handle. The water rippled around my ankles, as my legs shook. I gulped.

"What do you think will happen if one of those weird sucker-mouths grab us?"

"They might never let go."

I gaped, as the large group of suckers neared.

"Look," Jamie said, "If you're afraid of a few thousand little suckers, feel free to wait on the shore. It'll save you the trouble of having to use that cheap net."

I studied the large splashes, steadied my hands around the butterfly net's plastic handle and dug my soaked sneakers into the sediment.

The large splashes drew towards us. A moment later, they blended into the rapids. Jamie and I stared at the brown and white water. The water whirled between my legs, swirled around my ankles, foamed on my jeans, floated past my feet and tumbled down the creek. Beneath the foam and swirls, a sucker's fin drifted above the surface. Its body passed between my legs. Another sucker followed, and another.

"They're here!" Jamie shrieked.

The large splashes rose again. Suckers jumped above the rapids. Their bodies slammed into rocks. Thuds echoed above the creek's roar. Their snouts tried to grab the wet, algae-covered rocks. One tried to grab my jeans. I shook my leg, stumbled and steadied myself. My eyes strayed towards the sucker.

A small white tube lunged from its snout towards me. As I swatted my butterfly net towards him, a rapid grabbed him and pulled him down the creek.

Ahead of me, Jamie whacked the water. Suckers swam and jumped past him. Their brown fins skimmed the water's surface.

I felt a bump on my ankle. A sucker nudged me. A rapid carried him into a rock. His body slammed into the rock, stopped, and the long white tube in his mouth strained towards the river. Half of his body lay on top of the rock above the water. His black speckles shimmered in the sunlight and his brown scales dried. The fish's body shifted up and down, his gills opened wide and his large, black eyes stared down the creek.

Now's my chance, before Jamie catches one.

I waded through the rapids and stopped beside the sucker. Its body shifted on the rock, but it didn't move. I placed the small opening of the butterfly net in front of the sucker's white snout, lifted my sneaker out of the water and nudged its body. The sucker drooped into the water, but the net held its head. The orange handle bent and tensed in my hands. The sucker sucked on the mesh. Its tail flailed in the brown water.

"I've got one!" I screamed, "I've got one!"

Jamie swatted the water again. As the water splashed, he turned to me.

"No way. In that crappy net? Let me see."

Jamie waded across the creek and stared at the sucker, as it struggled inside the butterfly net.

"Whoa, that's a big one! Looks like you had it in you after all. Hold on, I'll grab the bucket."

Jamie stepped onto the shore and picked up the large plastic bucket off the slate. I looked down at the fish, as it sucked on the mesh and wriggled. I smiled. A moment later, I saw a group of suckers pass through the rapids and swim down the creek. I looked back at the sucker in my net. My lips drooped.

Jamie ran back into the water and stood beside me.

"Alright, one second there," he said.

Jamie tilted the bucket, skimmed a couple inches beneath the brown surface and scooped up the sucker from the net. He carried the bucket towards the shore, rested it on the slate, crouched, stared at the fish and laughed.

I stood in the middle of the creek. Suckers soared past my ankles and drifted into the rapids. My small hands dangled the empty butterfly net. Its thin mesh skimmed the brown water. I sighed. My lower lip trembled. I frowned. After a moment, I stepped through the rapids, landed on the dry slate and stood beside Jamie. I stared into the bucket. The sucker lay in a couple inches of brown water. Its body arched around the curve of the bucket and its snout gasped.

"That's a big one. Good job buddy!" Jamie said, stood and slapped my shoulder. I stared at the fish.

"We have to put him back," I said.

Jamie frowned.

"Why? We should keep him."

"Where?"

"In the bucket? Duh, where else?"

"The bucket isn't big enough."

"Sure it is. Look, his whole body's under water. We can give him a bit more, too, if it'll make you feel any better."

Jamie placed his hand on my shoulder.

"Besides, we need to show everyone in our class what a cool fish *we* caught. Maybe we'll set him free later."

I turned towards the creek's brown water, as the last few suckers from that large group floated down the creek, then I studied the sucker in the bucket.

"No, his family's going now. He needs to go with them."

Jamie laughed.

"There's no such thing as a "fish family." If we set him free later, I'm sure he'll know where he's supposed to go."

I turned towards the creek, as one last sucker whizzed across the rapids, slammed into the rocks and drifted down the creek. I shook my head.

"No, he's going now. I caught him, so I can let him go."

I grabbed the rough edges of the bucket, carried it to the creek's edge and tilted it. Brown water splashed into the river and a larger splash echoed across the creek. A moment later, the sucker swam across the brown water, tumbled through the rapids, slammed into the rocks and drifted down the creek. I smiled. The rapids roared. Foam drifted onto the shore.

The Fort

"You better hurry," Megan said, as the brown leaves crunched beneath her feet, "the thunder's coming soon." Megan sprinted into the forest. Jane followed. Her red hair flopped against her back. Leaves crackled and echoed behind them. I, twelve, stared at them through the bare, gray trees. Fourteen Mile Creek loomed, lurched and roared in the middle of the forest.

I turned to my left. A pile of sticks lay on the ground. I approached the pile, picked up a stick, rubbed the bark off and whipped the stick back on the pile. A raindrop landed on my hand.

How's this fair? Their fort was already built. I won't finish this thing before the storm.

The green chain link fence rattled. I turned and saw my dad. He stood on the other side of the fence in our backyard. His torn, dirt-covered, deer skin gloves rested on top of the fence.

"What're you doing there, Trent?" he asked.

I looked at the pile of sticks. Small water spots covered their bark. Megan and Jane's laughter echoed through the forest. I scowled.

"I'm building a fort before the storm comes."

My dad studied the gray clouds, frowned and nodded.

"So what's your plan?"

"I'm going to build a teepee out of these sticks," I said, as I pointed to the pile of sticks.

"A teepee?"

"Yep."

My dad snorted.

"Why would you do that?"

"Megan and Jane made one, so I want to make one too."

My dad smiled and shook his head.

"Where are you going to build this teepee?" he asked.

"Right where those sticks are," I said, and pointed to the pile of sticks again.

My dad laughed, shook his head again and said,

"Oh, boy."

He hopped over the fence. The chain link rattled. Raindrops crackled on the dry leaves.

"You can build a better, stronger fort faster than you can build a teepee," my dad said.

I gasped.

"Really?"

"Yes, come here."

I followed my dad. He pointed to two trees that stood four feet apart.

"See those two big trees?" he asked.

I nodded.

"These two will act as your foundation. Build your fort in between these two trees."

My dad pushed one of the trees. The tree stood still. My dad's hand recoiled.

"See?" he said, "half the work's already done by the forest."

My dad frowned.

"If it really starts to pour, though, make sure you get inside the house. Tell your sister too."

I nodded. My dad smiled, patted my back, walked across the dried leaves and hopped over the chain link fence. A black cloud floated above the trees and shadowed the forest. Thunder echoed in the distance. I stared at the two trees. After a moment, I studied the pile of sticks.

Now where do I start?

I sorted the four-foot long sticks in a pile and carried them over to the two trees. I stacked the four-foot sticks on top of each other. After a few minutes, a five-foot wall formed between the two trees.

Whoa! I built a stick wall! This is definitely cooler than Megan's stupid teepee.

I grinned.

I've pretty much built a log cabin.

I ran to my pile of sticks, flung my arms around them, dug my forearms into the dirt and dead leaves, pulled the sticks to my chest and carried them to my stick wall. I dropped the sticks onto the ground. Brown leaves rose. Mold filled the air. I sneezed. I stared at the stick wall and tapped my chin. Thunder echoed again.

Now what?

I studied the stick wall for another moment and gazed around the forest floor. A long, broken branch lay among the dead leaves. I ran towards the branch, wrapped my arms around its bark, dug my boots into the mud and dragged it back to my stick wall. A wind blew between the trees. Mist hit my cheeks. The leaves rose again. I dropped the long branch, picked it up again and leaned it against my stick wall. A few minutes later, I found another large branch. I leaned it against the stick wall. Raindrops landed on my forehead and pushed the sweat towards my eyebrows. My bark-covered hands trembled. I stared at the triangle framework.

Now it really looks like a cabin! I can't wait to show dad!

The black cloud merged with another black cloud. The tree's shadows darkened. I stared at the black cloud.

I need to finish this. Right now.

I grabbed thin sticks from the pile and lay them on top of the two angled branches. Rain spat on my hands. I threw leaves onto the fort. Leaves blew onto the roof. After a few minutes, the fort's roof covered the ground. I grinned, ran towards the fort, crouched and crawled through the small triangle opening.

Not very roomy in here.

A wind swept across the forest. Thunder echoed louder. Leaves and raindrops slammed against the fort. The twigs and branches on the roof tumbled and fell. A branch hit my head. I flinched and my head knocked more branches off the roof.

The roof collapsed on me.

After the wind settled and the rain eased, I brushed the sticks off of my body.

"Trent?" my dad called.

I stood, wiped the leaves off of my sweater and stared towards the chain link fence. My dad observed me. He frowned.

"What happened?" he asked.

I sighed.

"Well, I built a wall between the two trees like you said, but, when I leaned the other branches against it, the fort was too small for me to fit in."

My dad rubbed his chin and stared at the damp, ruined fort. He hopped over the fence.

"Find some bigger sticks that look like a Y," he said.

My dad picked up a small stick that looked like a Y and held it in the air.

"See, like this, but bigger."

My dad and I scoured the forest floor. After a few minutes, we each found a large Y-shaped stick.

"Now," my dad said, as he cleared the fallen sticks from the stick wall, "we'll stick the Y sticks in the ground opposite from the stick wall, okay?"

I nodded. My dad pressed the Y stick into the dirt. The forked end stuck up in the air. I stuck my Y-shaped stick into the ground a few feet away from his Y-shaped stick. We stared at the two Y-shaped branches.

"Now, grab one of those big branches," my dad said. I grabbed a big branch and dragged it to him. He picked up the large branch, placed one end on top of the stick wall and another on the Y-shaped stick. The Y-shape held the branch in place. He grabbed the other large branch, placed one end on the stick wall and rested the other end on the second Y-shaped stick. I studied the rectangular frame.

"There," my dad said, "now you've got more headroom. Just pile the sticks back on top and you'll be good for the rain."

"What about the thunder?" I asked.

My dad looked at the black clouds. He smiled.

"I bet this thing holds out through the thunder," he said, "but, if you ever have a doubt, you know the best fort is back in the house."

I gazed over the chain link fence and studied our two-story brick house.

My dad patted me on the back. He hopped over the fence.

I stared at the stick wall, the Y-shaped sticks and the large branches they both supported. My eyes drifted towards my pile of sticks. A wind blew through the trees, the leaves rattled and a raindrop grazed my hand. Megan and Jane's laughter echoed through the forest. Thunder rumbled.

The Ladder

"Quick, call the police!" my mother shrieked, "they've got the ladder, they've got the ladder!"

I, fourteen, gazed through the kitchen window, across the backyard and into the forest. The green chain-link fence rattled between the backyard and the forest. A moment later, three gray-covered bodies blurred among the pine and maple trees. I eyed the gray blurs, and then studied the "No Trespassing" sign attached to a maple tree.

My mother glared out the window, frowned and grabbed the cordless phone. Her pink slippers stomped across the hardwood floor. *The Young and the Restless* blared through the television. A few minutes later, blue and red lights flooded into the front hall. A door slammed. A knock echoed through the front hall and travelled into the kitchen. My mother opened the front door. A police officer stepped inside. He nodded.

"Now, run this by me again," the officer said.

My mother sighed.

"Three teens, on their lunch break I presume, walked into the forest to do whatever the hell drugs it is they do, approached our property, grabbed the ladder from over our fence, and then ran into the forest with it."

The officer frowned, scratched the scruff on his chin and placed his other hand on his belly. His belt creaked.

"The ladder?" he asked.

"Yes, the ladder."

Another police car drove down our street and parked in our driveway. The officer stepped out of the car, scanned the street and positioned his hands on his belt. His other hand rested by his cuffs.

The officer inside our house stared through the glass door at the second officer, nodded and turned back towards my mother.

"How do we get into the forest?" the first officer asked.

"If you walk up to Lakeshore Road and head towards the bridge you'll see a gate," she said, paused and pondered, "it'd probably be easier if you just jump our fence out back."

The police officer laughed. He placed his hands on his belly again.

"Look at me," he said, "Do you think I'm going to hop a fence?"

My mother grinned.

"We'll head around the block," he said.

The police officer stepped through the doorframe. He approached the second officer, pointed towards Lakeshore Road, tapped on his cuffs and spoke into his radio. The second officer grinned. After a moment, both officers walked towards Lakeshore Road.

I ran back to the kitchen and gazed across the backyard at the forest. The pine trees swayed against the green chain-link fence and the pine needles shimmered in the sunlight. A grey squirrel hobbled along the chain link fence and jumped onto a pine branch. A turkey vulture hovered in the sky. I gulped.

"Mom?" I said.

My mother stepped into the kitchen. She stood beside me and stared at the forest.

"Do you think those guys will get arrested?" I asked.

"I hope so."

I gasped. Sweat gathered between my toes.

"Why?"

My mother frowned.

"Well, for one, they stole our ladder. For two, they're probably down by the creek doing drugs or drinking."

I focused on a fingerprint on the kitchen window, and then I gawked at the hardwood floor. A piece of dried apple lay on the floor. I tapped it with my toe and placed my hands in my pockets.

"I'd hate to be those kids right now."

A few minutes later, a knock echoed into the kitchen. The front door creaked. My mother's voice muffled. I ran towards the front hall, my damp socks skid across the hardwood floor and my legs tensed. The first police officer stood in the doorframe. His hands rested on his belly. The ladder lay behind him on the front porch. He smiled and stepped outside of the house. My mother shut the door.

I ran down the stairs, leapt towards the front door, pressed my fingertips against the glass and stared at our driveway. My mother placed her hand on my shoulder. The first police officer approached his police cruiser. He spoke into his radio, sat in his police cruiser and drove towards Lakeshore Road. The second police officer's empty cruiser sat in our driveway. A grey squirrel ran underneath the car and gawked at me from behind the front tire. My palms sweat against the glass. My heart beat against my ribs. I stared at the empty second cruiser for a moment, and then I turned towards my mother.

"Mom?" I asked, "What's going to happen to those kids?"

Petro Park

"How the hell are we supposed to get out of here?" I asked
my girlfriend, Cydney, as we crouched between the maple
trees and the bushes at Petro Canada Park in grade eleven.
The moon shone above the trees and the trees hid us within
their shadows. A white car sat in the parking lot in front of us.
An empty beer bottle lay beside the car's front tire. Fourteen
Mile Creek meandered behind us. My eyes blurred, my body
stumbled, my hand pressed against a tree trunk and I steadied.
I studied the blue text on the white car. The text said, "Halton
Police." Cydney shook her head.

   "I'm not sure. How long do you think this guy's going to
sit here?" she asked.

I studied the white and blue police car again. Grey smoke drifted from the exhaust pipes and floated towards the amber streetlight. The headlights shone towards the long driveway that led out of the park.

"Hmm, can't be that long," I said and frowned, "Doesn't he have drunk teenagers he can go catch?"

"We are drunk teenagers."

"Yeah, but he doesn't know we're here."

"How do you know?"

Leaves rattled beside us. My head turned. I clenched Cydney's hand and Cydney clenched mine. A moment later, a grey squirrel appeared in the parking lot. I sighed.

"Is anyone still here?" I asked.

Cydney shook her head.

"I don't think so. As soon as the sirens started everyone ran into the trees."

"Well, we're still in the trees. How do you know no one else is?"

"I don't."

I stared into the police car's dark window. A man sat inside. The amber streetlight sifted into the car and reflected on his eyes. His amber eyes scanned the trees in our direction. I gulped.

My foot moved, my sneaker slipped in the mud, my worn down sole grazed an object and a clink echoed through the trees. My body froze. I stared at the man in the police car. His orange eyes still stared in our direction.

"What the hell was that?" Cydney whispered, "are you trying to get us caught?"

I turned towards her. Her gloss-covered eyes stared at me

and her lower lip trembled. I sighed and looked at the ground. An empty beer bottle rested in the mud. Mud covered its red and white Molson Canadian label. A low amber glow gleamed onto the bottle. I looked to my right and saw more amber glimmers in the mud.

"Oh, shit – " a boy's voice said.

A car door opened and slammed. Heels clicked on the asphalt. I turned and surveyed the amber-lit parking lot.

A teenage boy stood beside the white and blue police car. A black backpack slung behind his shoulders. His acne and facial hair shimmered in the amber light. He held a brown, glass bottle in his hand. A police officer stood in front of him.

"What're you doing in the park at this time of night?" the police officer asked.

"Um, I was –"

"You were what?"

I turned to Cydney.

"We're going to get caught. This cop's definitely going to sit here all night and wait. He knows we're here," I said.

"We're going to get caught if we keep talking."

"Well, what do you propose? Do you think we can just sit here all night and wait for him to leave?"

"Yeah, or we can walk out there and get busted like that guy."

I stared at the teenage boy. He held the brown bottle upside down. Brown liquid fell onto the asphalt, slid between the cracks on the ground, flowed into a metal grate and splashed in the sewer. Fourteen Mile Creek trickled behind us. I gulped.

"You don't still have that mickey of Captain Morgan's on

you, do you?" I asked.

Cydney placed her hand on the back of her jeans. She nodded.

"Drop it in the mud," I said.

"Are you crazy?"

"No, just drop it."

"No, this cost me thirteen bucks."

"I'll get you another one."

"I don't want another one. I have some here."

I shook my head.

"If you get rid of it, we can probably walk out of here and not get into trouble."

"How do you figure?"

"That guy's getting his booze poured out. If we don't have any booze on us, the officer will let us go."

"First of all, we're drunk. Second of all, we've been hiding in a bush. We'd probably get in more trouble than him."

I stared at the officer, as he wrote in a notepad. The booze on the asphalt reflected the amber streetlight.

"Look, Cydney, I don't want to get arrested. If he finds us in here hiding he'll be pissed. We should go out."

"No way, just stay here, we won't get busted. He'll probably leave after he deals with this dude."

The police officer handed the teenage boy a yellow piece of paper. The officer turned towards the trees. His amber eyes glared towards us. I gulped.

A moment later, a car screeched down the driveway and roared into the parking lot. Its headlights shone on the trees. My eyes caught the headlights. I stumbled and closed my eyes. The treads of my shoes slid and my knee dropped towards the mud. Cydney and I ducked lower behind the bush. She squeezed my hand and our hands sweat.

Brakes squeaked. A car door slammed.

"Cydney? Where are you? Cydney? Where the *hell* are you?" a woman's voice asked.

Cydney and I rose above the bush and stared into the parking lot. A black Toyota idled beside the police car. A woman paced around the lot. Her hands rested above her eyes and blocked the amber streetlight, as she gazed into the trees.

"Cydney, where the hell are you?" the woman shrieked.

The teenage boy and the police officer observed the woman. Cydney released my hand. She stepped across the mud and emerged in the parking lot.

"Here I am, mom."

I gawked at Cydney, her mom, the police officer, and her mom again.

"Get over here right now," Cydney's mother shrieked, "and where the hell is Trent?"

My body trembled. My teeth clenched. I stood, slid across the mud and emerged into the parking lot. Cydney's mother squinted.

"Trent? Is that you?" she asked, "both of you get over here!"

I lowered my eyes and followed the Toyota's headlights along the asphalt. When I reached the black Toyota, I opened the door.

Is the cop going to stop this? Is he just going to let us go?

I paused for a moment, and then I sat on the cloth-covered seats. The headrests and car radio spun. Cydney sat beside me. Her mother sat in the car and shifted it into drive. My

blurred eyes gazed through the window. The teenage boy and
the police officer stood under the amber streetlight.

The Night Heron

"Hurry! You're going to miss the coolest thing I've ever seen in Oakville," I said, as I, twenty-one, ran down Lakeshore Road in October 2012. My thirteen-year-old sister, Bridget, followed me. She wore a snapback cap, a flannel shirt, torn-up jeans and skateboard shoes. A camera hung around her neck. We sprinted across the cracked sidewalk, crossed the bridge and stopped beside a small dirt path. The dirt path led into the forest. A foxhole dipped on the edge of the path. I smiled.

"We need to go this way," I said. My heart beat against my chest.

Bridget stared down the foot-worn path, gazed at the foxhole and shook her head.

"You think I'm going down there?" she asked.

"Uh, yeah, you want to see something cool, don't you?"

A wind blew into the forest and the long grass bent towards the path. Fourteen Mile Creek's roar echoed through the pine trees. A car raced down Lakeshore Road. Bridget shook her head.

"We won't see anything," she said.

"How do you know?"

"Because this is a forest in Oakville. The most we'll see is a squirrel."

I grinned, shook my head and ran down the dirt path. Dust rose. Pebbles rolled. The long grass skimmed, scratched and tickled my fingers. The worn down soles on my shoes slid across the hard dirt. I reached the bottom of the hill, stopped, turned, stared past the long grass and trees and smiled at Bridget. Bridget stood on the sidewalk, tapped her foot on the concrete and shook her head. She sighed.

"Are you just going to leave me here?" she asked.

"I'm not leaving you, you're leaving me."

Bridget glared at me. A car sped down Lakeshore Road. Bridget shook her head and leapt down the dirt path. Her white sneakers slid across the dry dirt. Dust engulfed her white laces. I smiled, turned and walked farther down the path.

Large spruce trees sheltered us. Dead, grey branches rested by their trunks. Fourteen Mile Creek rumbled beside the path. Above the trees and the creek, the sun snuck through the pine needles and fragmented on the brown water. The brown water crystallized in the light. I turned to Bridget.

"Isn't it beautiful down here?" I asked.

Bridget wiped and wiped and wiped a cobweb off her jeans.

"No, it's irritating down here."

I studied the trees and weeds and grass and creek.

"You know, I used to spend a lot of time in here," I said.

"In where?"

"The forest."

I stepped on a dry branch. A crunch echoed between the pine trees. The creek's ripples softened.

"When I was a little younger than you," I said, "I used to come out here with my binoculars and look for birds."

"What kinds of birds?"

"All kinds. Crows, cardinals, robins, vultures. Sometimes I'd even see a hawk."

I pointed towards the river. A seagull stood on an algae-covered rock. Its orange beak pried a crushed Coke can.

"If I was lucky, I'd even get to see a seagull chewing on some garbage," I said and laughed. Bridget sighed.

"I came all the way down here to see a bird eat trash?"

I shook my head.

"Just wait."

We reached a bend in the path. I stopped. Bridget stopped beside me. I pointed above the long grass towards the creek.

"Let's go over there," I said.

Bridget stared at the long grass, looked at her dust-covered sneakers and sighed. I stepped into the grass. The long blades crumbled beneath my shoes. Bridget followed me.

We reached the edge of Fourteen Mile Creek. The creek trickled beneath us. My sneaker stepped towards the edge. A rock fell from the dirt, dropped into the water and sunk beneath the current.

"I don't think we should be near the river," Bridget said, "Mom's going to be mad."

I smiled.

"Nah, she won't. Not when you tell her what we saw."

I turned towards Bridget.

"Do you have your camera?" I asked.

Bridget placed her hands on her camera and lifted it towards me. I nodded, shifted towards the creek and crouched behind the long grass. Bridget crouched beside me.

"Now, we need to stay quiet," I said. Bridget frowned.

"Um, why?"

I turned to Bridget, grinned, gazed back towards the creek and pointed. A large bird sat in a dead tree on the other side of the creek. Blue feathers draped its head and wings, and white feathers covered its torso. Its long, large yellow talons clung to the tree branch. The bird's long, black beak pointed towards the rapids. Bridget's mouth drooped, as she stared at the bird. The bird turned and its red eyes studied us.

"Whoa!" Bridget shrieked, "That thing has red eyes! What is it?"

I placed my index finger in front of my lips.

"Shhh. It's a night heron."

"A night heron? Why is it called that?"

"They hunt at night."

Bridget nodded. She frowned.

"Why is it out during the day, then?" she asked.

I smiled.

"That's the beauty of this. I don't know why it's out."

"Why is that beautiful?"

"It's rare to see one of these things at all, let alone during the day."

Bridget stared at me. After a moment, she turned, lifted her camera towards her eye and twisted the lens. The camera's shutter clicked. The night heron studied the creek. The sun crept through the trees. A wind swept between the trees, shook the pine needles and tussled the long grass. The night heron's feathers furled. The creek rippled.

Float On

I Knew a Stranger

Who the hell is he, and where the hell did he go? I wondered, as I leaned against a green plastic table on Philthy Mcnasty's patio, sipped my beer and scanned the crowd for my old friend, Dean.

How can I not see him? The guy is like six foot three, six foot four now, I thought, but holy shit, I remember when he was like three foot one.

I turned to my friend Alan, as he drank from his beer and stared through his circular lenses across the dark parking lot at Speers Road. His slicked back hair shined under the patio's yellow light and red stubble lined his cheeks and sharp jaw line.

"Have you seen Dean?" I asked him.

"Nah, not since he was here a few minutes ago."

I sighed.

"It'd be nice to catch up with him some more," I said, "I haven't seen him since elementary school. I feel like I barely know the guy anymore, and he used to be one of my best friends, I think. He's a good guy, eh?"

Alan nodded.

"Yeah, he's a really good guy, man."

I remembered how Dean, a few minutes before, shouted my name, approached me like one of my best friends, introduced himself to Alan, lit a cigarette, asked me how high school had been at Blakelock, told me how high school had been at St. Thomas, discussed his love for film, said a few jokes, and then disappeared into the crowd.

While I pondered, Dean's voice rose above the canon of drunken banter on the patio, as I heard him tell a joke. I studied the drunk, blurred faces on the patio, as they laughed and drank from their beer bottles, and then I looked through the cloud of hair for Dean's ponytail. As Dean finished his joke, laughter filled the patio.

He must be here with a bunch of people. Maybe there are some other people here from elementary school, I thought and frowned. He's got to be the only six foot three, six foot four, guy in here with a ponytail and leather jacket on. How the hell don't I see him? I didn't recognize him when he approached me. I remember he always had short hair in elementary school, but damn, his new hair is sick. I want hair like that.

Streams of grey smoke swirled into the night air past the

patio light's glow and twirled towards the stars. I followed the individual streams of smoke down their spirals towards the cigarettes and the mouths the cigarettes sat in, but still I couldn't find Dean's mouth or cigarette amidst the crowd.

I can't believe I'm looking for Dean using cigarette smoke. I used to hang out with that kid when we were seven-years-old in his basement, and now he's smoking cigarettes. All I can picture is Dean in kindergarten, and, when I saw Dean light his cigarette earlier, I imagined a kindergartner lighting a cigarette.

The individual streams of smoke mixed together now in the summer breeze and a grey haze hovered above the crowded patio. Beer bottles clanked. Cab engines hummed from the parking lot.

Come to think of it, Dean *was* one of my best friends in kindergarten. I can't remember hanging out with him, though. But we *must* have hung out, I think.

I stared at the crowd for a moment, as laughter roared again above the shouts and banter, and then I shook my head.

Why can't I remember a damn memory other than hanging out in his basement? What the hell were we doing in his basement? Where the hell is Dean?

After a few minutes, Dean emerged from the crowd and spotted Alan and I. He smiled and walked towards us.

"Trent Ogilvie?!" he shouted, and then clanked his beer bottle with Alan's and mine and pulled a cigarette from his leather coat's pocket. He told a few jokes to us, and then I asked,

"Hey Dean, who'd you come here with?"

Dean looked around the bar.

"No one, man."

"Seriously?" I asked.

"Yeah, I just wanted to check out the bar."

I studied Dean's kindergarten, stubble-covered and aged face and I pondered,

Who the hell is this guy? I know his face so well. But shit, I would never go to a bar by myself. Was he always like this? Even back in kindergarten?

Dean told a few more jokes, and then floated into the crowd and disappeared under the grey haze and the patio's light. I stared at the drunken crowd. Dean's voice and laughter again rose over the dissonant bar chatter. I smiled.

Is this the kindergarten friend I knew? I wondered, and then I thought about the encounter with him earlier. To go to the bar by himself on a Friday night, just for the adventure, even though he could have known no one, is cool, but the fact that he came by himself and knew half the bar is an even cooler thing. But I guess that's Dean.

When to Write for the Dead

What the hell should I say? Or should I say anything? It can't be the Dean I knew. How? It can't be.

I trembled, as I typed Dean Cudmore's name into the Facebook search bar and clicked on his profile. As his profile appeared on the screen, a photo of a pickup truck appeared in the header and two large trains blurred in the background. A photo of Dean sat beneath the header in the profile picture section. His ponytail hung from his head, as he smiled. I stared at the photo for a moment, and then scrolled down the page. Wall posts appeared that said, "RIP," "Gone too soon," and, "Float on."

What does "Float on" mean? Why is everyone posting

that?

My eyes zoomed across the page, as I scanned the comments and wall posts.

How? I thought over and over and over again.

I returned to my newsfeed, as old, familiar names started to appear.

Chris knap… Taylor Palmer… Luke Kahnert… I haven't heard these names in a long time.

I opened Google and searched "Oakville News." The first headline read, "Man dies after being struck by GO train in Oakville." I opened the article and read, but the article didn't offer a name of the victim. I read another article, but still couldn't find a name. I returned to Facebook, opened the list of friends online and saw the names of my elementary school friends again.

Should I ask them? Is it bad to ask them how it happened? What if Dean *did* get hit by a train? I haven't spoken to most of them since elementary school. Are they going to think it's weird if I ask *them* when I haven't seen them in eight years? Is there no one I'm closer with that I can ask? It can't be Dean. What should I say? He was one of my best friends, I think.

I stared at Chris Knap's name.

Someone told me that Chris Knap thought I was a loser when I went to a different high school than them, and that he wanted to fight me. I don't know what I ever did to him. What's he going to think if I post something for Dean?

I stared at the names of my old friends for a while, and then I closed my Facebook, paced around my bedroom, opened my Facebook again and stared at the names.

Is there any harm in asking them?

I closed the list of friends again, and then stared and refreshed the newsfeed for a long time. As the night moved forward, my old friends posted memory after memory of Dean, and my old friends commented on each other's posts. I read each post.

Wow, they all still hang out. I haven't seen them in so long. Should I post something on Facebook? I feel like I should. Dean loved writing and I love writing too. How do I know that? Everyone here says he loved writing, so now I know he loved writing. Does that make a difference between whether another writer should write about the passing of a writer? I feel like it'd be the right thing to do, maybe. Why the hell can't I think of a memory?

For the next three days, after the family of Dean Cudmore created a memory page on Facebook for him, I watched my old friends and Dean's new friends post memory after memory of him, and the words "Float on" appeared again and again on the screen. My chest tightened, as I read them.

At one point, a video entitled "Float On" popped up in my newsfeed. The video started and the song "Float On," by Modest Mouse, roared through my speakers. In the video, Dean, as a high school student, created a banner with the words "Float On" on it, ran around the school and gave the banner to as many students as possible. All of the students smiled, as they held the banner. I smiled and watched, as Dean united the entire school through his video. After the video ended, I stared at the tribute page again.

I wish I'd been there for his "Float On" video. I wish I was *in* the "Float On" video. I *need* to say something. All I have is this vague memory of him as a kid. I think it was the first time I went to someone's house without my parents. Dean and I stood in a basement, his basement, I think, but I can't remember what we were doing. What the hell were we doing? We were so young. I can't write about that memory. There *must* be more memories.

I sighed, held my tense fingers above the keyboard and stared at the computer screen.

I could write about that time I ran into him at the bar back in the summer. Was it this summer or last summer? Does it matter which summer it was? What if I say it was this past summer but it was really the one before that? Am I lying? Does it matter? There still would be a truth to the writing, right? I'm writing for Dean, so nothing else should matter, right?

I stared at the dust and smudges on my computer screen for a while, breathed in deep and nodded.

Ok, I'm going to write something. I have to. I'll feel better when I do.

I typed in the comment box on Dean's memory page for a while. As I finished, I edited the memory two or three times. I stared at the blue "comment" button. My finger hovered above the mouse pad. After a moment, I clicked on it. My paragraph on Dean appeared on the memory page. I stared at the paragraph and my body loosened. I closed the computer and turned to my schoolwork.

I wonder if any of my old friends will "like" my post.

I refreshed my Facebook page every twenty minutes in search of "likes" from my old friends.

After a day or so, some friends from high school and people I'd never met "liked" the post. I sighed, re-read the paragraph, and then, as I moved my curser to the exit button, a small heart in the comment box appeared from the founder of the memory page.

I Watched, as the Tears

Will I weep with them? I wondered, as I walked down the red carpet along the side of the church. Will I even sit with them?

Below the large crucifix and granite alter, a photograph of Dean sat on an easel between two bouquets of flowers and Dean rested in a small cremation box. In the front few rows of pews, in front of the photograph and box, Dean's family sat. I turned my head forward and stared at the pews to the right of Dean's family. My old friends Chris Knap, Taylor Van Der Doelen, or, as we called him in elementary school, TVD, and Taylor Palmer, sat and stared straight ahead. Their kindergarten faces looked the same, except stubble now grew from their cheeks and time and grief weathered their faces. I looked

at Chris Knap's long hair, white bandana, thick beard and
the small red bump beneath his nose he'd had since we were
young, as I approached the pew and thought,

Should I sit with them? Will they accept me like they
did when we sat together at school assemblies, or has something changed since I switched schools? There's Chris Knap, I
wonder if he still wants to fight me. He wouldn't snub me at a
funeral, would he?

As I stepped towards their pew, Chris turned to me first
and nodded. He stuck out his hand, as his tear-drenched eyes
stared at me. I grasped his hand and he grasped mine firm.

This is the Chris I knew ten years ago, except I've never
seen him sad. I wonder if I look sad to him.

I nodded at him, and then turned to his left. TVD looked
at me, forced a small smile and extended his arm towards
me. I stared at the two metal spikes that now protruded from
his eyebrow, and then I shook his hand too. After, my old
best friend Taylor Palmer turned to me, shook my hand and
hugged me. He held me for a moment, as his body shuttered,
and then he lifted his tear-soaked cheeks, released me and
forced a small smile. My chest tensed. I sat with my mother in
the pew behind and studied my three old friends. I watched,
as the tears trickled between the stubble on their kindergarten
cheeks.

Why am I not crying with them? I'm sad, I know I am,
but why don't I seem as sad as them?

After a few minutes, more people filed into the church
and another old best friend of mine, Nathan Bonifacio, walked
towards the pews, said hello to everybody, and then sat with
his family in the front of our section of pews. A woman from

Dean's family's section wailed and wept and her cries echoed off the large ceiling. The priest walked towards the altar and the choir sang the opening hymn.

Maybe when the funeral starts I'll remember Dean better. Maybe then I will weep with my old friends.

As the funeral progressed, I searched the words in the readings, gospel and sermon for my past connection with Dean, but still I couldn't find it.

After the funeral, everyone in the church rose and spoke to one another. My mother turned to me.

"Ready to go?" she asked.

I stared at my old friends, as they gathered their coats and talked to one another. The sun poured through the stained glass windows and green and red fragments of light sparkled on their tear-soaked cheeks.

"I should say good-bye to everyone," I said, "It might be the last time I see them for a long time."

I approached Nathan. His eyes shifted towards me.

I wonder if he recognizes me. I don't want an awkward stare.

"Trent…?" he said, "Trent!"

A smile formed on his face, as he threw his arms around my shoulders and hugged me.

"It's good to see you man," he said, as he held me tighter, "It's good to see you."

I exhaled.

"It's good to see you too, man."

After a moment, he released me, rested his hands on my shoulders and smiled. He studied my old face. I smiled back, and then turned and faced Chris Knap. He paused in his conversation and approached me.

"Thanks for coming man, they're having a reception at the Knights of Columbus just down the street. There's going to be guitars, an open mic and food. You should come by. I don't know how long it's going on for, but I think we're going to head over there in a half an hour or so."

I nodded my head.

"Of course I'll be there man."

Wow, Chris Knap invited me. I never thought that would happen.

I looked around the church at the faces of my old friends.

I have to go. I have to be there with them.

Chris shook my hand again, and then I turned and walked towards the church's exit with my mother. On my way out the door, Taylor Palmer and TVD hugged me again, thanked me for coming, and then my mother and I emerged into the sunlight in the church's parking lot. I looked back at the church and thought,

They accepted me, but why didn't I cry with them?

EXO

I know everyone going to this, I thought, as I approached the Knight's of Columbus Banquet Hall, but I'm about to walk into a room full of strangers.

The sun shone over the building and spread across the car-lined street. Chris stepped outside the building, pulled a cigarette from his coat's pocket, put the cigarette in his mouth and lit it.

This is a weird sight. All I can picture is Chris as a little kid and now he's got a cigarette in his mouth.

Chris stared at me and exhaled. I walked towards him. He stood with Dylan Glover and someone I didn't recognize.

Is he going to be a dick to me now? Is he going to talk

to me or just shrug me off now that the funeral's over? He
was nice to me at the funeral, though. He was the first one to
shake my hand.

Chris nodded at me, as he brought his cigarette to his
mouth again. I stared through the smoke at the small pink
bump beneath his nose that I remembered from elementary
school.

"Where'd you come from?" he asked.

I turned and pointed at my white Subaru far down the
industrial road.

"Way down there. I didn't even bother looking for parking in the lot because the street already looked packed."

Chris laughed and nodded.

"Yeah, you know what? I went to the CIBC behind the
building beforehand, and honestly, after I saw the parking lot, I
decided to just leave my car at the bank and hop the fence."

"That's smart," I said, "I didn't even think to try another
parking lot."

"So what are you doing now?"

I shoved my hands in my black pant's pockets and my
sport coat crumpled around my arms, as a cold wind blew
across the front of the brown, brick building.

"I go to U of T for English and Professional Writing."

Chris lowered his cigarette and nodded.

"That's neat man, do you commute?"

"Yeah, but I take my classes at the Mississauga campus so
it's only a twenty minute drive."

"Nice man, that's not bad at all."

I nodded.

"What are you doing now?" I asked, as Chris's Facebook

profile page drifted into my memory, "Your're at UBC right? How do you like it out there?"

"I *was* out there. Honestly, it was beautiful man. The nature and wildlife there is incredible and the city is fantastic."

I pondered for a moment and thought,

My old hockey buddy, if I remember from Facebook correctly, goes to school in BC. I'll name drop him.

"An old buddy of mine, Taylor Macintosh, goes to school out there, do you know him?" I asked.

"Yeah I do, man. He goes to Simon Fraser, which is pretty close to UBC."

Alright, good, I thought. We have mutual friends. Sort of. I haven't spoken to Taylor in years either. Don't we already have mutual friends from elementary school? Why am I worrying about this?

"I'm not at UBC anymore, though," Chris said, "I'm up in North Bay doing nature conservation."

I gaped at Chris, as he placed his cigarette on his lips amidst his thick beard.

This guy wanted to fight me, and now he's conserving nature. What the hell is going on?

"That's sweet, man," I said, "really random, but I like that a lot. I wish I was doing something in nature."

"Yeah man, it's awesome. The program's really hands on too. We do work with animals every day giving them shots and things like that."

"That's awesome, it must be beautiful out there, too."

"Oh yeah man, it's incredible. The wildlife is amazing."

Chris threw his cigarette on the ground and walked towards the door.

"We should go inside and see everyone."

I followed Chris into the lobby. A small child wandered, smiled and spun around beside a full coat rack. I stared passed the child into the crowded, dim banquet hall and sighed. Chris walked ahead of me and disappeared into the hall. He joined a group of my old friends.

I wish I was still talking to Chris, I thought, as I identified the childhood faces of my now adult friends. Just find someone you know first, Trent, and then start from there. There has to be someone here from my high school. Dean knew people from Blakelock.

I squinted, entered the hall and weaved through the crowded, circular tables, as people drank beer from red cups, coffee from white cups and snacked on triangular sandwiches and wraps.

A middle-aged man in a black suit approached me. I recognized his face. He shook my hand.

"It's nice to see you," he said, "It's been a long time. Say hi to your mom and dad for me."

"I will," I said. The man walked past me.

Who the hell was that? Dammit, I know that face.

I walked along a food table and ran into my friend Sonia Silano. Sonia and I drifted after elementary school but regained contact within the last few months. I approached her. She turned and looked at me. Her long, dirty blonde hair waved past her cheeks, as her sunken eyes and lips faced me. She set down her plate of food and hugged me.

"How are you doing?" I asked.

She paused. Her tear-lined eyes stared at me, and then she nodded.

"I'm ok."

We talked for a moment, and then she invited me to her table. My old friends Luke Kahnert, Justin Garvey Donnelly, or, as we called him in elementary school, Buck because of his buck teeth, and TVD sat and talked to each other. As I sat down, none of them turned towards me. I sighed. Sonia introduced me to her friend Jessica.

I wonder if they think it's weird that I'm here. I used to snowboard with Justin in grade eight. We formed a snowboard team. Who the hell else was on that team? Why isn't he acknowledging me now? Should I say something to them? Why haven't they said something to me? These were my good friends in elementary school - some of my best friends - so why are we sitting here like this?

Sonia, Jessica and I chatted for a while, and then Dean's friend Mike stood in front of the room and spoke. The room silenced.

"You know the first time I really grew close to Dean," Mike said, "Was this one time I was walking in Toronto and, all of a sudden, I heard this yell, "BAM BAM! MIKE HYNES!" and so I turned and, sure enough, it was Dean Cudmore yelling at me from a car, and then a moment later, Dean proceeded to jump and roll from the moving vehicle, which, I later found out, was owned by a family that Dean had just met at the station who had offered him a ride."

The room erupted in laughter. Mike continued.

"That night we went to a party and found a forty of booze, so we did the only logical thing you do when you find a forty of booze: we took it, left the party and proceeded to get wasted out of our minds. After we'd gotten wasted and everyone else had left, Dean and I were walking home and we started discussing what it would be like to be homeless. A few minutes later, low and behold, Dean pulled a garbage bag out of a garbage can, both of us took off our shirts, and then we proceeded to lie on the freezing cold concrete and fall asleep under the garbage bag. When we woke up in the morning from our hangovers and, well, being close to hypothermia, we realized that not only was our puke covering the garbage bag, but the bag we used as a blanket was *filled* with someone else's puke."

The crowded room cringed and laughed.

"But I guess that's just another night with Dean."

Mike proceeded to tell more adventurous stories about Dean and the room laughed and laughed, and then Mike's tone shifted to a serious one and his words resonated in me.

"You know," Mike said, "The night Dean died he was tagging his film company's name on a train. His company's name was "EXO," and, for those of you who don't know, "EXO" refers to the planets outside of our solar system, and Dean chose this name because he truly thought that, if all humans in the world could love one another and unite, we could reach the exo planets, and he believed that this union was possible through film."

As Mike finished his speech, I pictured Dean, as he stood on the tracks, held his spray can and painted "EXO" on the railway car beneath the solar system and the solar systems beyond, and then my mind travelled into the dark night sky, soared up towards the trillions of small, bright lights and weaved past each individual star towards the exo planets of Dean's dream, and then, after a moment, I drifted back into my seat at the round table, as my old friends, Luke, Dylan, Justin and TVD, turned towards me and spoke.

I Wept, as the Memories

Will there be tears tonight, will I feel sad, or will I remember my memories of Dean?

I surveyed the bar, Less than Level, with Alan and Sonia, and then spotted my old friends Luke Kahnert, TVD and Justin Garvey Donelly, as they sat with their parents. I saw the middle-aged man that asked me to say hello to my parents at the reception.

Whose dad is that? He must be one of theirs. I hope they turn towards me. Didn't they see me walk in? I guess I could go over there, but I don't want to interrupt. Why won't they turn towards me?

Chris left the group and walked towards the bar. He spotted me, said hello and we spoke, as he ordered a beer. After the bartender handed him his beer, he turned to me.

"My dad's here, eh," Chris said, "Say hi to him at some point."

I turned towards the table and saw Chris's dad. His bald-head shone in the dim light. His thick, grey and white beard stuck off of his cheeks, as he tilted his head back and drank his beer.

Wow, now there's a familiar face. Mr. Knap. He looks the exact same, but older.

I sighed and turned towards Chris, as he shifted towards the stage.

"Alright let's go see your da-" I murmured, but Chris didn't hear. He walked towards the stage. Alan still stood be-side me. I turned back towards Luke, Justin, Mr. Knap and the other parents that sat at the small round table, clenched my teeth and frowned.

If I walk over there, I'm going to have that awkward moment where none of them know who the hell I am, and then we're all going to be standing there awkwardly, as I try to explain who I am and how they know me, and then I'm going to look like an idiot. I wish they'd all just remember me. I talked to Luke and Justin briefly at the reception though. We both used to snowboard together, I remember that.

I exhaled and walked over to their table. Mr. Knap studied me, as I held my hand out.

"Do you remember me?" I asked, as I lowered my hand towards the ground, "It's little Trent Ogilvie from elementary school."

Mr. Knap gaped. He shook my hand.

"Wow, you look different," he said and laughed. His gaze stayed on me.

After we spoke, I approached the middle-aged man from the reception. He shook my hand and told me to say hello to my parents again. He brought Luke up in conversation.

Of course! This is Luke's dad. How could I forget him with a face like that? He looks like an older Luke.

I frowned.

But Luke looks old now too.

Mr. Kahnert told me he was a writer and I told him how I aspired to write too. He gave me a website for writers that he volunteered at and told me to contact him whenever I wanted advice on writing. I thanked him and left the table.

Alan and Sonia joined me. We walked towards the stage in the corner. Around the stage, a large group of young adults nodded, as a man played acoustic guitar and sang. When he was done, a psychedelic instrumental band performed. We all drank more beers. At the end of their set, the guitarist pulled a microphone from the side of the stage and spoke.

"This last one's for Dean, so I want to see all of you dancing and singing along," the guitarist said. Within a few seconds, the riff from "Hey Ho, Lets Go," by the Ramones, spilled from the speakers into the bar. The crowd erupted, danced and bumped into each other. I scanned the crowd for my old friends, but I didn't see them. As the music reverberated through my body, I clutched the damp neck of my beer and ran into the crowd. Random bodies smashed into my torso and legs. I spilt beer onto my jeans. The crowd's limbs, the band on stage and the dim lights overhead blurred and mashed, as my head twisted and bounced to the rhythm of the song. The smooth soles of my desert boots slid on the beer and various liquids on the hardwood floor. I smiled and stumbled. More beer fell onto my jeans.

As the song ended, the guitarist said, "Float on, Dean, float on." The crowd quieted and stepped back from the small, triangular stage in the corner. I sipped from my beer and found Alan and Sonia. I stared at Sonia's face, as her lips drooped and tears ran down her cheeks. Her arms swung around my shoulders and her torso slumped against mine. Her body shifted up and down, as she sobbed into my shoulder and, every few moments, gripped me tighter. My eyes closed, as my chin rested on her shoulders. The chatter of my old friends and the bar crowd mangled together and entered my ears. Sonia released me. Mascara ran down her damp cheeks. She forced a smile and joined her friend Jessica across the bar.

I turned to Alan and he sighed. We turned towards the stage, as three men and my friend Taylor Palmer jumped on stage. Within a few minutes, a hip-hop beat bounced through the speakers. The four of them rapped about smoking weed. My old friends Justin, Luke and Chris walked onto the dance floor, stood on the other side from me and watched them rap. I observed Taylor in his flat brim hat, as he clutched the microphone and rapped for the crowd of old friends. His large wristwatch glimmered in the spotlight and his other hand bounced up and down to the beat.

I remember Taylor used to beat box, but I never thought I'd see him rap.

I turned to Alan and laughed.

"They're pretty good, eh?"

Alan nodded.

"Yeah man, they ain't bad."

When the rap set finished, my friend's TVD, Luke and Justin stood in a circle. TVD nodded at me and I walked over. Alan stood still and sipped his beer. I turned towards my three old friends.

"It's been good to see you guys, it's been a long time," I said, "we should hang out sometime and keep in touch."

TVD pulled out his cellphone.

"Let's exchange numbers so we can actually make this happen."

TVD, Luke, Justin and I took out our phones, exchanged numbers and texted each other.

"I miss you guys," I said, "We used to be really good friends."

TVD put his phone away and turned to me. Luke and Justin turned to me too.

"We still are your friends," TVD said.

I smiled, as my teeth clenched and my eyes tingled. I hugged each of them. TVD and Luke walked towards the bar. Justin stayed and talked to me.

"Man, do you remember," Justin said, "When we used to snowboard with Dean back in grade eight, and we made up Team Ripshift?"

I gaped.

"Dean was a part of Team Ripshift?"

"Yeah man."

How could I have forgotten that? We used to snowboard together all of the time. I think he even came up with our team name. We made a video of us snowboarding too. I'm pretty sure he videotaped me running into a skier.

"I completely forgot," I said, "That's so cool. I remember we thought we were the best."

Justin laughed.

"Yeah man, we *thought* we were the best."

Justin walked towards the bar and I thought,

So Dean and I weren't just friends when we were really young. How could I've forgotten that we were good friends in grade eight? That wasn't even that long ago. We used to snowboard all of the time together. How could I've forgotten that?

Taylor Palmer approached me from the stage.

"I'm so happy you came to all of this, man," Taylor said and hugged me. He released me, smiled and walked into the crowd. I walked to the left corner of the stage and found Nathan Bonifacio, as he wound a microphone cable. He turned to me and smiled.

"Trent…"

Nathan threw his arms around me and hugged me like he'd hugged me at the funeral. He said my name over and over again, as he clutched me tighter. After a few minutes he released me and smiled.

"So good to see you, man," he said.

"Good to see you too, man," I said. We exchanged phone numbers. Nathan stood, hugged me again and disappeared up the stairs.

I turned, threw on my red lumberjack coat and walked towards Alan. I stared around at the empty pool tables, cleared dance floor and closed down bar, as my friends placed their coats on, hugged one another, sobbed and comforted each other, and then one by one walked out of the bar.

This is how it is, I thought. The faces of my youth, the

ones I recognized when I had no cares in the world, and the ones that I still recognize, and the ones that I will recognize forever, have been brought together to mourn the face of somebody that I will forever recognize, and somebody that everyone here will forever recognize. Dean. I can still see his face as a child, when we used to play as kids, and I can see him on the snowboard hill now, as we filmed videos before he created "Float On" and EXO, and we thought we were the best, and I can still see him at the bar only a few months back with his ponytail, and even then his face didn't seem changed. These faces. My world consists of faces, and these faces are the faces of my innocence. All of these people were part of my innocence, and now a part of that innocence is dead. I don't want to lose any more of it. Justin's buck teeth. The red bump beneath Chris's nose. These faces. The faces of my old friends, as they walk out the door. The faces of my new friends. The face of my dead friend. These faces that I will never forget.

I turned to Alan and my mouth dropped. He stared at me and opened his arms, as my arms shook and my head fell to my hands. Tears poured from my eyes. My palms shook my face. Alan grabbed me and I pressed my hands harder to my eyes. I wept, as the memories floated back into my mind. I remembered not just the Dean I knew, but also the friends I knew. Alan patted my back. Another hand rested on my back. I removed my hands from my eyes and turned my red and damp cheeks towards the figure. Sonia stared at me and smiled.

What the fuck is happening? I didn't want this to happen in front of anyone. They don't need to see me like this, not after this long. Why am I crying? I miss my friends. They don't need to see me like this. That's the last thing they need. I miss my friends.

"I'm sorry," I said.

"It's ok," Sonia said, "It's alright to cry."

I tried to stop, but my hands cupped my eyes again. Alan held me harder. My body shuttered.

"I miss my friends," I said.

Float On

When I remembered death, and I struggled to compile Dean's memories, as they fragmented in my head,

When Alan and I followed a brick path in Burlington along the lake's crumpled shoreline a few days after Dean's funeral, as a wind grazed our hands and fingers and we approached a split in the path, in which the right path led towards the main road and the left path led through the bushes,

When we followed the bushes down the rough path, emerged onto a stone, shell and garbage-covered beach, heard the shells crumple beneath our feet and our soles sunk into the sand,

When I looked above the sand dunes to my right, saw

smoke twirl from a smoke stack in the air, and then remembered Dean's kindergarten face, as he smoked a cigarette,

When I showed Alan a tree, whose branches swooped towards the sand, and then rose above the lake water,

When we climbed the tree, sat on the dry bark and stared down the shoreline, past the metal transformers and power lines, at the Skyway Bridge,

When I looked down at the water, as small waves rolled towards shore, rose, peaked, fell and disappeared back into the lake's body,

When Dean's ponytail and his aged, kindergarten face formed in my head, and then faded,

When Chris's, Taylor's, Justin's, TVD's, Luke's and every other elementary school friend's scruff-covered faces formed in my head, and then faded,

When the waves beneath my feet rose again and again, and then faded again and again, but looked the same, and different, each time,

When the pink sun kissed the earth's arc and painted pink lines across the dark lake,

When the dark lake rose again, covered in pink flakes of light,

When I turned to Alan and thanked him for helping me, and he patted me on the back and said, "always,"

When the sun stared at us for the last time of the day and the waves faded to a soft roll and splash against the wet sand on the shore,

When Alan and I gripped the dry bark, climbed down the tree, walked along the broken shells and garbage along the dark beach, passed through the rough path and emerged on the brick path under the city lights,

When I turned to Alan, as the wind hit our faces again, and said,

"I miss everybody, and not just the people from this weekend, but everybody I've known in the past,"

When Alan turned to me, patted me on the back and said,

"It's just time, man, it's just time,"

And when we stopped and stared at the black lake where the waves of today, and the waves of the uncountable years before, rose and fell the same and different each day, and then rested in the still night air,

Then I remembered life, and I knew that Dean's memories, wherever they rested in my mind, floated on forever.

Acknowledgements

Guy Allen, for reminding me to activate my verbs, write in a notebook every day and utilize the long sentence. And the short sentence.

Laurel Waterman, for encouraging me when I discarded two months worth of work to write the stories for Float On.

My family, for supporting me in not just my writing, but in all endeavours I've ventured into.

Patricia Ogilvie and Alexander Tkachuk, for reading and editing my stories over and over again.

Dean Cudmore, for your friendship, legacy and message of hope.

Trent Ogilvie grew up in Oakville, Ontario. He graduated from the University of Toronto with a specialization in English Literature and a minor in Professional Writing. When he's not writing, Trent enjoys driving old cars and drinking coffee. This is his first collection of short stories.

Made in the USA
Charleston, SC
07 April 2014